Why You'll Love This Book
By Jeremy Strong

Clever, brave, funny and always the optimist, Little Wolf
quickly wriggles his way into your your heart and stays there.
Lurching from one perilous adventure to the next and living
on his wits, Little Wolf manages to remain winningly bouncy
about Life and Living.

At the same time he also provides us with delightful
observations concerning family and relationships. Ian
Whybrow has created a real classic with this gem of a story
and Tony Ross's drawings provide a perfect match.

This is one of the best blinking blunking books I've read.
Definitely.

Jeremy Strong

Jeremy Strong has written over eighty books,
including severalbest-sellers and award-winners, such
as *The 100 Mph Dog* and *BewareKiller Tomatoes*. He
spends much of his time visiting schools and festivals
world-wide to entertain and inform children and to
encourage their own reading and writing. He is
particularly keen to pass on the joy of books to young
children in the hope of starting up a lifetime's habit.

D1150846

Also by Ian Whybrow and illustrated by Tony Ross

Little Wolf's Diary of Daring Deeds
Little Wolf's Haunted Hall for Small Horrors
Little Wolf's Postbag
Little Wolf, Forest Detective
Little Wolf's Handy Book of Poems
Little Wolf Pack Leader
Little Wolf's Big Book of Spooks and Clues

LITTLE WOLF'S BOOK OF BADNESS WON THE BIRMINGHAM
CHILDREN'S BOOK AWARD 1996

U.K.R.A. BOOK AWARD WINNER 1996
FOR MAKING A SUBSTANTIAL CONTRIBUTION
TO CHILDREN'S LITERACY

First published in Great Britain by Collins in 1995
This edition published by HarperCollins Children's Books in 2009
HarperCollins Children's Books is a division of HarperCollinsPublishers Ltd,
77-85 Fulham Palace Road, Hammersmith, London W6 8JB

The HarperCollins website address is
www.harpercollins.co.uk

1

Text copyright © Ian Whybrow 1995
Illustrations copyright © Tony Ross 1995
Why You'll Love This Book copyright © Jeremy Strong 2009

Mixed Sources
Product group from well-managed
forests and other controlled sources
www.fsc.org Cert no. SW-COC-1806
© 1996 Forest Stewardship Council

FSC is a non-profit international organisation established to promote the
responsible management of the world's forests. Products carrying the FSC
label are independently certified to assure consumers that they come
from forests that are managed to meet the social, economic and
ecological needs of present and future generations.

Find out more about HarperCollins and the environment at
www.harpercollins.co.uk/green

Little Wolf's
Book of
Badness

Ian Whybrow
Illustrated by Tony Ross

HarperCollins *Children's Books*

The Lair, Murkshire

Dear Bigbad

I have had no reply to my many letters to you. I therefore have no choice but to send this one by the paw of my eldest cub, Little Wolf. I want you to be his teacher.

Little is a bad boy at heart, I am sure, but he is worryingly well-behaved at the moment. He has been far too nice to Smellybreff, his baby brother, and only yesterday he went to bed early without being growled at. His mother and I think that it is time he left the Lair and had some adventures. We want him to go to Cunning College to learn his 9 Rules of Badness, and earn a BAD badge, just as you and I did long ago at Brutal Hall.

We are at our wits' end. You are our only hope. We rely on you to make a beast of Little Wolf.

Your anxious brother,

Gripper

> ### WARNING!!!
> THIS PAPER HAS BEEN TREATED WITH SPECIAL POWDER THAT WILL SHOW UP THE PAW PRINTS OF ANY SMALL BEAST SNEAKING A LOOK AT IT.

Dear Mum and Dad,

Please please PLEEEEEZ let me come home.
I have been walking and walking all day, and
guess how far? Not even ten miles, I bet. I have
not even reached Lonesome Lake yet. You know
I hate going on adventures. So why do I have to
go hundreds of miles to Uncle Bigbad's school in
the middle of a dark damp forest?

You say you do not get on in life these days
without a BAD badge. But I know
loads of really bad wolves who never
went to school. Ever. Like my
cousin Yeller for one. I know you
want me to be wild and wicked
like Dad, but why do I have to go
so far away? Just what is so
wonderful about Cunning College in
Frettnin Forest? And what is so brilliant about
having Uncle Bigbad as a teacher? Is it all

because Dad went to Brutal Hall and they made him a prefect and he got a silver BAD badge when he left? I bet it is.

There is another four days' walk, maybe more to Frettnin Forest. Let me come back and learn to be bad at home.
PLEE-EE-EEZ!!!

Your number 1 cub,

Little Wolf

PS Don't forget to say Hello baby bruv to Smellybreff and tell him not to touch any of my things.

By Lonesome Lake
Day 1 – night-time

Dear Mum and Dad,

I am a bit lost.

I think I have come to Lonesome Lake just where the River Rover runs up to it. I used Dad's map as a tablecloth for my picnic lunch. Now it is hard to tell if you have come to a river or a bit of bacon rind.

I have not had word from you to return home, so I must continue on this stupid long journey, even though I might never find Uncle Bigbad. He never answers Dad's letters. Maybe Cunning College is closed, and he has moved from Frettnin Forest. Anyway, how will I know I have found him when I do?

WANTED

BIGBAD

HUGE REWARD

I have got the Wanted poster that you gave me, but it is years old. Maybe he has changed. What will he look like now? Too scary, I bet!

Just now the sun fell in the water. I did not like it. Now the moon has come up and I can just see my pen and paper but I wish it was brighter. My tent is stupid. It falls down all the time, so I have curled up in my rucksack. Camping is my worst thing, and maps too. I am frozz, I am hopeless.

Yours tiredoutly,
Little Wolf

Up the hilly end of Lonesome Lake
Day 2 – morning

Dear Mum and Dad,

I woke up this morning feeling a bit tickly with ants in my rucksack. They were small but plenty of them, and quite tasty for breakfast. Then I was more cheery. I started walking soon after the sun jumped out. It was hiding behind a hill.

3 hours later.

I have stopped now for a rest and one of Mum's rabbit rolls. Yum yum, only 25 left, worse luck. Shall probably starve… You know I am a hopeless hunter.

You just think I am a goody-goody, I bet. Is that the reason why I have to go away for badness lessons? But I told you I only cleaned my teeth last week for a joke. And brushing my fur, and going to bed early, that was just to trick you! You ask my cousin Yeller, it was his idea. He said let's *pretend* being good. I just said OK. Then you were s'posed to say, "Oh no, Little Wolf has gone barmy." Then I was s'posed to say, "Arr Harr, tricked you, I am a bad boy really." But no, you would not listen, you did not understand. You said I must go to Cunning College, I must live in Frettnin Forest until I get my BAD badge and learn Uncle Bigbad's 9 Rules of Badness.

I bet you won't make Smellybreff leave home when he is my age. You will just say, "Oh yes, my darling baby pet. You stay here safe with us and watch telly all you want." And what about Yeller? I 'spect you think he is a small bad wolf but no. You do not see him doing good things like I do. Like the kite he made for me to take with me, with yellow wolf-eyes painted on it. And sometimes he says pardon when he burps, too. Bet his mum and dad are nice and do not send him to school in a faraway forest.

Yours fedduply,
Little Wolf

Dear Mum and Dad,

Aaah, the hunters got me in Lonesome Woods, urg.

Only kidding, I am all right really. Had you worried though, eh?

Walked miles today and have got to Spring Valley, but still a long long way to go. Have eaten most of Mum's rabbit rolls already, book, shame. I can smell your present for Uncle Bigbad, lots of lovely mice pies. Yum, yes please, scoff scoff (not really).

I wonder if Uncle is as greedy as you said. Hope he is not ~~crool~~ cruel, I am only small. That reminds me. Tell my baby bruv Smellybreff not to chew my teddy bear or I will chew him back.

Dad's map is a bit wrong because there is no big black monster between Lonesome Woods and Murky Mountains. I looked and looked but it is only trees here. Off to Roaring River tomorrow.

Love from

Little Wolf

PS. Oh dear, it was not a big black monster on the map. It was a squashed ant, sorry.

Dear Mum and Dad,

I am writing this under a bridge at a town called Roaring River. This makes six bridges I have crossed on my journey, and still not even in Beastshire yet. I am sure it is much much further to Frettnin Forest than Dad said.

Spent last night in a bus shelter. Quite warm and unscary, with my torch switched on going flash. Mum always says yellow eyes are friends with the dark. True, but it is still nice to have a torch when you are a small loner.

Roaring River is too big, not a good place to wake up. There are so many human people here you would not believe. It is not safe for cubs.

Yours witchingly,

Little

Dear Mum and Dad,

Spent the day in Roaring River. I like the cars, they are nice and smelly and good growlers. And buses are best of all. They go FSSSHHH when they stop and the people line up and get inside them. It is funny, just like Dad eating sausages.

This morning I wanted to try being a sausage. So I got in a line behind a large woman at the bus stop. Then guess what, she hit me with her shopping just for wearing a fur coat. She said,

"Take that for animal rights." I said, "Stop, I *am* an animal!" She said, "What sort?", so I told her and she ran off screaming, har har.

Her shopping was quite tasty except for some white powdery stuff in a box. It made your tongue go bubbly…

Yours spottily,

Little Wolf

Dear Mum and Dad,

I was glad to leave Roaring River. Feel a bit better after a good gargle in a stream, and all the nasty froth spat out at last.

Got to Crowfeet Crossroads by noon. Nice houses here, but not as nice as our smelly cave. Did not see any people, only a post box to post this.

I had a think today. Do you know what? Everybody else thinks I am bad, even if you think I am a Goodie-4-Paws. Remember when Mum was asleep that time and I nipped off her whiskers with the claw clippers? And what

about when I glued Smellybreff's tail to his high chair? So whyo Y do I have to make this stupid long journey?

Just now I thought I heard Yeller calling me. It was only a train howling in the valley. I am going now up the steep and wiggly path through the Murky Mountains. It looks VERY dangerous. Hope you are satisfied.

Farewell from

L Wolf

Dear M and D,

I had some big shocks today.

You did not say about how
cold it gets up in the
mountains. You have to climb
up and up above Crowfeet
Crossroads. Sometimes you are
up so high that nothing grows,
not even trees. And the ice
makes your feet slip. Two times
I nearly skidded right over
the edge of the path. It was
terrible. When I peeped over,
the houses down below looked
small as sparrow nests.

Then I got lost. I followed one thin path. It
just went round and round and came back
where I started. So I wrote TRICK PATH in big

letters on a rock for the next traveller. And off I
went fedduply.

Just before dark I found the edge of
Murkshire. I felt sleepy and wanted to lie down.
My breath was in white clouds. Then I saw a
deep dark tunnel going into a mountain wall and
a sign above the entrance. It said

BORDERLANDS TUNNEL
NO 'U' TURNS
NO STOPPING
NO WAY BACK
FRETTNIN FOREST – 58 MILES
THE SCARES START HERE

My fur started jumping up all along my back. But I did not want to stay in the open and freeze. So big breath and in I went, running, running. I shouted, "Can't scare me. Yellow eyes are friends with the dark!" Then guess what! My words shouted back — only louder and growlier! I ran and ran with my puff hot in my throat. I had just enough puff to get to the end. It was the best feeling ever to be in the open, looking at the moon shining down. It was shining on the village of Borderlands Market.

And that was how I got here.
Just.

Can't keep awake. More tomorrow.

Dear Mum and Dad,

Guess who woke me up this morning? I will give you a clue. He has got sharp eyes, a pointy face, red bristly fur and a small like pepper.

I was all curled up under a small cart near a street light in the market square – zzzz – fast asleep. All of a suddenly, I felt hot breath in my ear and this voice saying, "My boy!" I jumped up and banged my head. I tried to run but strong paws held me down and then I yelled, "Ooo-er, a fox!"

The fox said, "Mister Twister is my name. You are camping under my stall." I said, "Whoops, sorry, Mister Twister." he said, "Do not worry yourself, my boy. There will be no charge. For now. But then, something tells me that you are a keen young chappie who is eager to assist me with my work today."

I did not know how to say no to him. More later.

Yours stuckly,

Little

Dear Mum and Dad,

Yesterday I did work in the market for Mister Twister. He sells dizgizzes (cannot spell it). My job was putting on false beards, masks, sheep's clothing, etc. and walking up and down saying, "Hey, guess what I am?" It was quite good fun dressing up, and loads of people stopped to buy things.

A small mouse came up to me and he said, "I am lonely. Can you sell me something to help me make friends?" I said, "Yes, I can. Here are some tie-on wings. Wear these and stand on your head. Then loads of bats will come and

play with you." And guess what? He bought 2 pairs!

And my best thing was finding something for a stoat to wear to a fancy dress ball. I sold him half a coconut and told him to shave all his fur off. Then he could go as a tortoise! He was so pleased he said I could keep the change.

I like being a market worker.

Yours richly,

Little

Dear Mum and Dad,

Mister Twister said I was a good worker and would I stay? I wanted to but I told him I had to go to Cunning College and study for my BAD badge. "You amaze me!" he said, and his sharp eyes went wide, and his red fur went even more bristly. "Do you mean to tell me that you are going to Cunning College in Frettnin Forest?"

I said, "Yes, do you know it?"

He said, "My boy, I was a teacher in that school many a full moon ago! Your uncle and I used to be partners! Can you really be the nephew of that nasty mean bad horrid crook?"

I said a proud "Yes".

The fox told me more. He and Uncle Bigbad met ages ago in Broken Tooth Caves when they were both hiding from the police. Uncle had the idea to stay out of sight in Frettnin Forest and start a school for bad beasts. He promised Mister Twister that if he worked hard, teaching the naughty pupils everything he knew, he would soon be rich.

Mister Twister said, "My boy, it was dreadful. The pupils never gave me a moment's peace! They were most awfully sly and squirmy, all those little skunks and stoats and rattlesnakes and cubs! How they got on my nerves, those spoilt little brutes! And what a fuss their horrid parents made, always wanting to know when their ghastly offspring would be getting their BAD badges! They quite wore me out. But when I asked your uncle for some money, just enough to allow me to take a short holiday, he threatened to eat me!"

I said, "What did he say?"

Mister Twister said, "He told me to get out

and he said that if I ever put a paw in his school again, he would boil my bones and serve me up as soup."

I said, "Oo–er!"

The fox said, "So you see, your uncle is a miser and a cheat. He has bags of money hidden away but he will not part with a penny of it. You would be unwise, my boy, to leave Borderlands Market. What is more, Frettnin Forest is a SHOCKING place, dismal, dark and lonely. Your Uncle Bigbad is dangerous. He has a terrible temper. In short, he is Mister Mean. My strong advice to you, my boy, is STAY AWAY FROM CUNNING COLLEGE!"

I said, "Yikes, you have got a point!"

Yours having a good think,

LW

Dear Dum and Mad,

I am a bit confused and bothered. Mister Twister wants me to stay with him for ever and be his dresser-upper. Sometimes I think Oh yes, nice idea because one day I could have a stall of my own. Next thing, I think Yes, but what about learning the 9 Rules of Badness? If I do not, how will I get a BAD badge and keep up the good name of Wolf?

But Mister Twister has got me worried about Uncle. I mean, about boiling him up as soup. If he is going to make soup out of his large friend, what will he make out of a small nephew he has never met? Will I be his special pupil or just a sausage in a sandwich?

Yours nervously,

Little

Dear Mum and Dad,

I have decided. I am going on. I think I like adventures now. (A bit, anyway.) Tell Smells and Yeller for me. It will be a good shock for them.

I slipped away from Borderlands Market very early before Mister Twister came and talked softly to me. I did not trust his voice. I have still got the bonnet he gave me for dressing up as an old lady. It might come in handy.

Borderlands Market and the mountains are far behind me now. Today was my longest walk ever. One good thing, the land was flat, but no shade for miles and miles. On the map, it is called The Parching Plain and now I know why. The track was dusty and the sun was hot. I was longing for a stream to splash my tongue in but no luck. I wished I had brought a snowball from the mountains to lick.

In the afternoon, some big birds came, big as planes. They glided round and round. The slower I walked, the lower the birds flew. About 4 o'clock one came close enough to show his hooked beak and claws.

Then I remembered Yeller's present, my kite with the yellow wolf-eyes painted on. I had to stop to get it out of my rucksack and fix it together. Now the birds came so low I could see their shadows flick on the stones near me. I howled to make them stay back and then I was ready.

I tugged the string and the kite FLEW up. I flipped and flapped it right in their ugly faces. You should have seen them scatter! It was like tadpoles in a pond when you plop in a pebble!

Don't forget to tell Yeller. I kept his kit flying right across The Parching Plain and not one bird bothered me again.

I am posting this just on the edge of Frettnin Forest. I have not gone in yet but tomorrow I will have to, worse luck. Oo-er. It looks darker in there than the Borderlands tunnel.

Good thing I can whistle, eh?

Yours chinupply,

Little W

Near Cunning College
Frettnin Forest

Middle of night after
Day 10

Dear Mum and Dad,

I have arrived. It took me all day what with the paths so overgrown. But I have found Uncle's school at last. The fox was right. This IS the shockingest, dismalest darkest part of the forest.

Much too late to ring the bell. If I wake up Uncle now he is sure to eat me.

I have tried putting up my tent but no good. So I have made a small lair in a bush in the college garden, OK but a bit prickly.

Oh no, now it is drizzling here! Sorry about the smudges. I wish I was curled up under my nice dry rock at home.

Talk about spooky. So overgrown, with eyes

and croaks and squeaks everywhere! Good thing
I have got my torch. I am holding it in my
mouth to see what I am writing. Also, I can
point it and light up a sign by the door of the
schoolhouse from here. It says

CUNNING COLLEGE.
BADGES AWARDED FOR
WICKED WAYS
DIRTY DEEDS
& BAD HABITS.

Gosh, sorry about that. Something
went WOO, made me jump. This is SO scary, it
stands your fur up.

Not sure when I will find post box but I just
want to say something. OK, I did teach my little
bruv I Love Little Pussy. And Christopher Robin
is Saying His Prayers with actions, I admit that.
But that was just tricks, honest. You know I am
not really nice and polite. I do not usually brush

my teeth and fur either. You ask Yeller. I just hope Uncle isn't too cruel. I do not want to get boiled.

This could be my last letter.

Ever.

And it will be all your fault.

Yours damply,

Master L Wolf

PS   Smellybreff can have my ted but I promised Yeller my box of tricks.

Dear Mum and Dad,

Guess what, not dead yet!

Woke up this morning so damp and frozz, I thought blow it, be brave, better be boiled than die of frozz. So I went ding ding on the bell.

Next thing, boom boom, big feet coming down the hall, loads of huff and puff. The door went *eeeee-aaaaah* and there was Uncle Bigbad, all tall and thin and horrible. He is not like in the Wanted poster. His eyebrows are furry like caterpillars and they join in the middle. He is very fierce, and he has got great big red eyes and great big long yellow teeth and great big long streams of dribble dribbling down. He reminds me a bit of Dad, but hungrier. And he wears a great big gold BAD badge on his chest.

So I took a big breath to get steady but my voice went wobbly. "H-h-h-hello Uncle Badbiggy, I am your n-nephew L-little Wolf. M-Mum and Dad sent me so you can t-teach me the 9 R-Rules of B-Badness."

He snarled his great big horrible snarl and he said in his great big horrible posh voice, "GGGRRR! BEGONE VILE BALL OF FLUFF! FLY AND FLEE OR I SHALL FETCH OUT THE VACUUM CLEANER AND HOOVER YOU UP OFF MY FRONT STEP!"

I said, "B-b-but I am your nephew, L-little W-Wolf. Didn't you get Dad's l-l-letters?"

He said, "GRRRR, I HAVE CEASED TO RECEIVE LETTERS."

I said, "Why?"

He said, "BECAUSE THE POSTMEN
WILL NOT DELIVER. JUST BECAUSE I
DEVOURED 1 OR 2 OF THEM! IT IS NOT
FAIR, I AM ALWAYS STARVING THESE
DAYS! IN FACT, TALKING OF FOOD,
STAND STILL A MINUTE WHILE
I PUT SOME SALT AND
PEPPER ON YOU!"

I said, "Wait, Uncle, do not devour me, try
some rabbit rolls! I think I have 2 left. They are a
bit stale, sorry, but tastier than me."

He said, "GRRRRR, GIVE THEM TO ME
SWIFTLY, SWIFTLY!" Then he grabbed them
and banged the door in my face, bang.

Gulp, I am coming home.

Yours trembly,
Littly

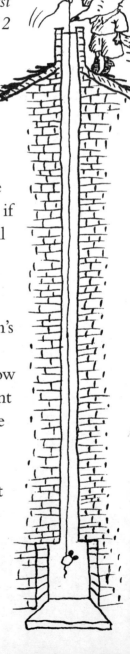

Frettnin Forest
Day 12

Dear Mum and Dad,

I started going back along the forest path, running, running. I felt misery – no BAD badge, no lessons, nothing. Then I thought, Oh no, the shame, what will Mum and Dad say if I go home now? Oh boo, now I will have to camp out for ever, which is my worst thing.

THEN. Ding, I had an idea, Mum's mice pies that she made for Uncle's present! I hid half the pies in a hollow tree. Then I turned round, and I went creep creep to the college again. The letter box was too small, so I went round the back and climbed on to the roof. I got 1 mice pie and tied it to a long string off my kite (good old Yeller!). Then I let it down the chimney.

Next thing, I heard Uncle say,

"SNIF SNUFF SNY!
    I SMELL PIE!"

And then Uncle's great big long tongue went
SLIP SLAP. You could hear him going mad
looking for pies, crashing the furniture about. So
I jiggled the string. All of a sudden WOOOOOF,
gone! No more mice pie.

Next I let down a little note, it said

And guess what?

I am IN.

Your brainy boy,

L Wolf, ESQ

Day 13

Dear Mum and Dad,

What a shock when I first went inside!
Cunning College was empty except for Uncle
and dust and cobwebs everywhere. Not one
pupil was left in the classroom. I said to Uncle,
"Where are all the pupils?"

CUNNING COLLEGE FOR BRUTE BEASTS

He said, "DEPARTED, SCATTERED! I AM
SO *FRIGHTFULLY* FRIGHTENING THEY
ALL FLED AND FLEW AWAY! NOW GIVE
ME MORE PIES, GGRRRRR! SWIFTLY,
SWIFTLY!"

What could I do? I gave him one and down it
went, GLUP. Then he said,

44

"MORE PIES, MORE! GGGRRRRR!
SWIFTLY! SWIFTLY!"

So I said, "If I give you 1 more mice pie, will
you be my teacher?"

He did not listen, he only swallowed the pie,
GLUP. Then he said,

"MORE, MORE I MUST HAVE MORE!
MORE MICE PIES OR I'LL EAT YOU!"

I said, "But Uncle!"

He said, "BUT WHAT!!" and he PUFFED
and he HUFFED.

I thought Oh no, he will kill me dead. But I
got my braveness up. I said, "There are lots more

pies hidden in the forest! You can have them *but*, teaching first, pies after."

And guess what, he went all nice! He said, "OH MY DEAR SPLENDID HANDSUM NEPHEW, PLEASE LET ME TEACH YOU BAGS OF BADNESS."

He says we start lessons tomorrow. And tonight I am sleeping in the *dorm*!

Yours proudly,

Little

PS   How do you like the posh notepaper?

Day 14

Dear Mum and Dad,

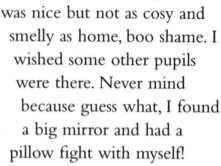

Slept in the dorm last night. It was nice but not as cosy and smelly as home, boo shame. I wished some other pupils were there. Never mind because guess what, I found a big mirror and had a pillow fight with myself!

I got up early and did grrrrs for the practice. I have got a bit of a sore throat now, but I think I am quite scary. Then I sharpened my pencils and colouring-in crayons and pointed them all the same way so I was ready for class.

My first lesson that I learnt today was this. Small wolves clean up, big wolves sit down and watch telly.

Bit sad, eh? I thought we would be doing Badness, but now. Uncle got huffy and puffy and said all his pupils must clean the blackboard, flit the flies, polish the desks, shoo the spiders, and scrub the floor, windows and lavs.

So I did. It took me a long time, nearly till dark. Uncle said, "GRRRR, WHY ARE YOU SO SLOW, YOU SISSY?"

I said, "I am not slow but everything is filthy dirty."

That was the wrong answer. Uncle sent me to bed and ate my supper.

Yours hohummly,

Littly

Day 15

Dear Mum and Dad,

No cleaning today, hooray! And guess what, I have learnt 2 Rules of Badness already!

I found a quite clean notebook in one of the desks and I wrote in it

Uncle came in the classroom. He was shining up his big gold BAD badge with his sleeve. I said, "Hum nice! When will I get my badge?"

Uncle was nasty, he said, "NOT UNTIL YOU KNOW THE 9 RULES OF BADNESS AND THAT WILL TAKE YOU YEARS AND YEARS BECAUSE YOU ARE NOT CRAFTY ENOUGH TO FIND THEM OUT SWIFTLY."

I said, "Maybe not, but I am still going to try my hardest."

Uncle said, "VERY WELL, MY CLUELESS CUB, LET US START WITH A STORY WHICH MIGHT HELP YOU OUT. 2 RULES OF BADNESS ARE HIDDEN IN IT, BUT YOU ARE MUCH TOO SMALL AND HOPELESS TO FIND THEM!"

I said, "Never mind, tell me the story anyway."

So Uncle smiled his big horrible smile and he began.

"ONCE UPON A TIME THERE WERE 3 LITTLE PIGGIES AND THEY GOT ON MY NERVES SINGING THAT THEY WERE

NOT AFRAID OF BIGBAD WOLF. AND
THEY KEPT GOING HA-HA-HA-HA-HA
ALL THE TIME. SO I HUFFED AND I
HUFFED AND I PUFFED THEIR HOUSES
DOWN AND ATE THEM."

I made a joke. I said,
"Gosh, Uncle, fancy
eating their houses!
Were the bricks tasty?"

Uncle said,
"SILENCE, SPECK!
THAT IS NOT FUNNY! GGRRRR, I
ONCE HAD A BLARSTED DREADFUL
ACCIDENT WITH A BRICK HOUSE. I
NEARLY BLEW MY HEAD OFF TRYING
TO HUFF IT DOWN. SO YOU BLINKING
BLUNKING KEEP QUIET ABOUT BRICK
HOUSES!"

I said, "Well now I think I can make a guess.
I know what Rules 1 and 2 are, Uncle! The
answer is:

RULE 1. HUFF AND PUFF A LOT.
RULE 2. SAY LOADS OF RUDE WORDS."

Uncle got very angry. He said,
"GGGRRR! HOW DO YOU KNOW
THAT? YOU MUST HAVE CHEATED!
SOMEBODY TOLD YOU THOSE RULES!"

I said, "Nobody told me! I guessed!" And I
wrote Rule 1 and 2 in my Book of Badness.

He went, "GGGRR!" and bit a lump out of
the sink.

Love from

Littly

Day 16

Dear Mum and Dad,

My 3rd day at Cunning College, and Uncle has stopped my lessons. He said there was nothing in the larder and I must go for food. I said, "Do you mean go to the shops? They are miles away."

He said "SILENCE, MOANER! I HAVE NO MONEY, THEREFORE YOU WILL HAVE TO HUNT FOR OUR LUNCH IN FRETTNIN FOREST. BRING ME BACK A SQUIRREL BURGER, SWIFTLY, SWIFTLY."

I thought, funny, didn't that fox say he had bags of money hidden somewhere?

Oh dear, I spent ages trying to catch squirrels but I am hopeless at climbing trees. All I got was just some peabugs and earwigs for crunchy snacks.

Uncle went mad for a bit when I got back. He growled and kicked the stuffing out of the sofa. (He was quite scary but no more than Dad.) Then he ate the crunchysnacks and went to bed. He says it is new moon tomorrow, therefore he must get his strength up.

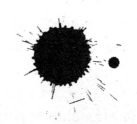

He would not even stop to tick my work in my Book of Badness, so not much Badgework yet. But do not fret and frown, I will soon be the baddest boy in the pack.

Yours youbettly,

L

Day 17

Dear M and D,

Boring boring boring. The most interesting thing today was it rained. Here is a poem I wrote called BORING SNORING.

It's raining it's boring
Uncle Bigbad is snoring
He howls all night
And he looks such a sight
And he never gets up when you call him.

This is a pic of me trying to wake him up.

 CUNNING COLLEGE FOR BRUTE BEASTS

Dear Mum and Dad,

I feel like running away. It is rubbish here. No other pupils to play with, nothing to do, nothing to eat and you do not even get letters because of Uncle eating the postmen. I am starting to wonder if he is as brainy as he keeps saying he is. I have not learnt a thing except huffing and puffing and no new rude words either. I could stand it if Yeller was here to talk to, or even Smellybreff. I am a very lone wolf.

I have not seen much of Uncle since I took him his breakfast in bed. I said to him, "Here is your nice breakfast, now can you teach me the 3rd Rule of Badness?"

He said, "DO NOT DISTURB, I MUST SLEEP ALL DAY AND STAY AWAKE ALL NIGHT."

I said, "Doing what?"

He said, "BEING A TERROR!" And then he said, "FLY AND FLEE, SMALL FLUFFBALL. GO OUTSIDE AND DO SOME QUIET HUFFING PRACTICE."

I did what he said, I huffed and puffed in the garden but it made me giddy just blowing dandelions.

Yours fedduply,

Little

Day 19

Dear Mum and Dad,

It is gone midnight and I cannot sleep. Uncle is on the roof, howling and howling at the new moon. He goes on and on. He is not being a terror, just a pain.

I cannot stand it.

Please let me come home and I promise *promise* I will never read another book, I will stick crayons up *my* nose more often, I will be rotten to Smellybreff and hide his spoon and pusher all the time, I will be a real ~~noosunce~~ ~~newsens~~ pain. Only don't make me stay in this blunking blarsted silly college. (See, I can say lots of rude words now. Can't you just be proud of that?) I cannot bear another night of Uncle's howling.

Yours ~~despritly~~, desperately,

Littly

Day 20

Dear Mum and Dad,

Guess what, we had a visitor today, thrill thrill. It was a tall man with a berry on his head and a whistle on a string. I thought yippee, somebody to try my ggrrrs on. I opened the door (eeeeee-arrrrrr) and did my best ggrrrr.

He patted me on the head and said, "So sorry to bother you, sonny him, but we are camping nearby. Could you possibly do something to mend the burglar alarm that kept going off last night on your roof. My poor cubs never slept a wink. Good morning."

I said, "Fly and flee immediate-lee!" But he did not seem to notice, he just saluted and said, "Thank you very much, sonny jim, have a nice day."

He did not fool me with that story about cubs. No way he is a wolf. I wonder what trick he is up to.

I cannot ask Uncle, he is asleep again. Ah, well, must go and look for something to pounce on, I am starving.

Yours peckishly,

Littly

Day 20
Night-time

Dear Mum and Dad,

Guess what, just when I thought, Oh no, I will never learn any more Rules of Badness, I found out Number 3!

This is what happened 1st thing today. Uncle was up on the roof. I was having a good sniff round the kitchen, looking for a snack. And do you know what? I found *loads* of food. There was ratflakes, some dried vole, even half a moosecake! They were hidden in the back of a cupboard, and Uncle said there was no food in the house! The fox was right, he *is* a miser!

It made me stop and wonder. Perhaps Uncle has got some hidden treasure somewhere, after all!

I did not have time to search because all of a suddenly, Uncle came down off the roof. Such a bad mood! He told me it was a waste of time howling because the moon cheats. He said, "IT COMES NEARER AND NEARER BUT JUST WHEN YOU HAVE HOWLED YOUR HEAD OFF AND YOU THINK IT IS CLOSE ENOUGH FOR YOU TO TAKE A NICE BIG CHEESY BITE OUT OF IT, IT BACKS AWAY!"

Then he crawled into bed all grumbly.

Thus and therefore Uncle was fibbing! He was not trying to be a terror, just trying to get a free snack! What a greedy guts!

So guess what, I do not think Uncle always tells the truth. And that is how I found out Rule 3. I wrote it down in my Book of Badness.

RULE 3.   FIB YOUR HEAD OFF.

Yours sherlockholmesly,

Me

Day 21

Dear Mum and Dad,

Bit tired today. I could not sleep because of thinking about the man with the whistle. Do you remember, he came to complain about Uncle being a burglar alarm? I have not told Uncle about him yet because I have got an idea. I am going to play a trick on that man, and then Uncle will most likely think, AHA! THAT IS A BLUNKING BLARSTED GOOD TRICK, SO NOW I MUST TEACH THAT CRAFTY NEPHEW OF MINE LOADS MORE BADNESS.

My best idea so far is, stuff something up the man's whistle. Crafty, eh? But I am still trying to think of something even badder than that. See? I am trying my hardest to be like Uncle, so you can be proud of me.

I looked all over the forest to find the camp where the man said he keeps his cubs, but no luck yet. Still, I found a cottage not far from here. A girl lives there. I watched her all morning to see if she would be fun to play with, but not really. She is too busy dressing up in red riding hoods and taking picnics to her granny, etc., boo shame. I am quite surprised Uncle has not eaten her yet. But maybe he has noticed that her dad is a woodcutter with large muscles and a big sharp axe.

My best news is, the girl took her dad a picnic and guess what, she dropped 2 chicken legs out of her basket, yum yum!

I am saving them (big secret).

Your crafty

Little Wolf

Day 22

Dear Mum and Dad,

I gave Uncle one of the chicken legs I found and that made him be in a really good mood. So I said to him, "I know where there are lots more."

Then I got my book out and I said, "Uncle, I have written down 3 rules in my Book of Badness. Can you teach me Number 4?"

He said, "PERHAPS, BUT HOW MANY MORE OF THESE DELICIOUS CHICKEN LEGS CAN I HAVE?"

I said, "One now, Uncle, lots more later." (Only one really but I was thinking of Rule 3, fib your head off.)

He said, "I ADORE CHICKEN LEGS SO I WILL TELL YOU 2 RULES!"

I copied them carefully in my Book of
Badness, like this:

RULE 4.   IF IT SQUEAKS, EAT IT.
RULE 5.   BLOW EVERYBODY ELSE.

This is easy cheesy!! Soon I will know all 9
Rules of Badness.

Petit wolf (French)

Day 23

Dear Mum and Dad,

I keep on at Uncle to teach me more Rules of Badness but he has got very snappish. He just says HUFFING AND PUFFING all the time and I know that one. Also he has moved the food in the kitchen to a new hiding place, I think he thinks I have been nibbling (I ask you, would !? hem hem).

Yore puzzled

Littly

Day 24

Dear Mum and Dad,

Got another Rule, hooray! It is
RULE 6.   DO YOUR DIRTIEST EVERY DAY.

Uncle has got a big mirror in his room, all nice and dusty. He spent 4 hours yesterday gazing at himself and he must have just scribbled it in the dust without noticing. (He loves himself *so* much!)

Quick as a chick I put it down in my Book of Badness. Then I decided to go exploring and see if I could find anybody to do my dirtiest on. I went through Frettnin Forest and right over Dark Hills, looking for the man with the whistle and his cubs. And guess what, I found their camp down by Lake Lemming!

Sad to say, I could not think of a good trick to

trick them. But I did do a trick on a beetle today. I said, "Hello, sonny, would you like to play a game?"

So he said, "OK, why not?" So I said, "Go on then, say, 'What is the time, Mister Wolf'."

So he said, "Why?" So I said, "You will see in a minute." So he said, "OK. What is the time, Mister Wolf?" and I said, "DINNER TIME, har, har!"

He was quite tasty.

Wait till Uncle hears that, he will make me a prefect, I bet!

Your best cub (tell that to Smellybreff, he will go mad, har har),

Little

Cunning College for Brute Beasts

Day 25, I think
(just my luck if it is wensdie
I can not spell it!)

Dear Mum and Dad,

I told Uncle about tricking that beetle yesterday. He did not make me a prefect, he got all jealous instead. He said, "GGGGR – RRRUBBISH, THAT IS NOT WICKED, THAT IS A GOODY-GOODY TRICK!"

Being a bit upset, I went out for a wander in the forest and guess what, I bumped into the man with the whistle! He said, "Hello, sonny jim. I am the leader of a pack of cub scouts. We are camping down by Lake Lemming. Tomorrow we plan to have a barbecue. We hope you can join us. Here is an invitation." I snatched the invitation and

CUB SCOUT BARBECUE 7 o'clock by LAKE LEMMING

said my scariest GGRRRAAH but he said, "Oh dear, have you got a sore throat, sonny jim? Have a cough sweet, must dash now."

I ran back and told Uncle. He said, "A CUB SCOUT BARBECUE? YUM YUM, I LOVE CUB SCOUTS, DELICIOUS."

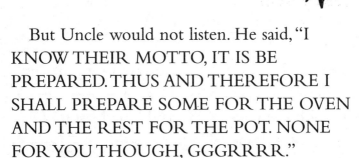

I said "Uncle, I think the pack leader wants us to go and eat his *sausages* not his cub scouts."

But Uncle would not listen. He said, "I KNOW THEIR MOTTO, IT IS BE PREPARED. THUS AND THEREFORE I SHALL PREPARE SOME FOR THE OVEN AND THE REST FOR THE POT. NONE FOR YOU THOUGH, GGGRRRR."

Boo shame, Uncle is too good at doing the dirty.

Yours upsettly,

Little

CUNNING COLLEGE FOR BRUTE BEASTS

Dear Mum and Dad,

Had an outdoor lesson today, learnt Rule 7 and Uncle bit me.

At 1st Uncle was in a good mood because he was plotting. He decided to catch the cub scouts by a trick called charming. (Have you heard of it? Nor had I.) Anyway, Uncle showed me how you do charming on a mole.

We went to this field all covered in mole hills. I said, "What are we doing here, Uncle?"

He said, "I AM SHOWING YOU CHARMING. SO SHUT UP, YOU SISSY FLUFFBALL, OBSERVE AND LEARN FROM THE MASTER."

I watched and took notes. First he lay flat on his tummy. Then he smiled a big horrible *smile*.

Then he shouted down the mole hole,
"GGGRRRR! LISTEN, MOLEY, COME
OUT OR I WILL BASH YOUR HILLS IN!!!"
And lastly, he took a running jump and skwish,
he skwished the mole hill with his great big
horrible feet. I made notes in my Book of
Badness like this

How to do Charming:
    big smile,
    running jump,
    skwish hills

I added:

Say horrible growly things about bashing.

There were loads and loads of hills, uncle took
ages jumping on them. And do you know what?
We never even saw the mole. He was hiding
underground.

I said to Uncle, "I think charming is rubbish."
That is when he went mad and bot my bittom.
(Other way round, sorry.)

He said, "WAIT TILL YOU SEE ME
CHARMING THOSE CUB SCOUTS
TOMORROW!"

Yours sorebottly,

Little

(nice pic of a mole, eh!)

Day 27

Dear Mum and Dad,

What a muckupp! Uncle is in bed with a headache and he did not catch one cub scout to eat, not even a sausage. I will tell you about it.

Uncle sat and cooled his sore feet in a bath in front of the fire al morning. Suddenly he said, "AH, NOW I AM READY FOR SOME PROPER CHARMING." He drank his bathwater, burped and dried his feet on the curtains, then off we went to Windy Ridge. It was just before the sun hid.

It was frozz up on the ridge, it made your teeth ache. Uncle said we had to smile a big smile and stand in the North wind till it got stuck. It took *ages*. Then we had to kerlump through the forest in the dark and take our smiles to Lakeside Meadow.

Talk about hard, finding it in the dark, and we were glad of the warm campfire. Uncle stood frozz in the firelight looking all horrible, like he had his tail caught in a gate.

The pack leader came up to us. I thought, Oh no, trouble.

But he said, "Welcome, sir, welcome, sonny jim, would you like something to eat?"

I was going to say I would have a nice hot sausage but Uncle smiled his stuck-on smile and said, "GGRRRR! YESSS! GIVE ME YOUR CUB SCOUTS OR I'LL HUFF AND I'LL PUFF AND I'LL BLOW YOUR TENTS DOWN!"

The pack leader shouted, "Quick, boys, emergency!" He blew his whistle and bing, all the cub scouts jumped into their tents and zipped up.

Uncle huffed and he puffed his hardest. Nothing happened. The tents dented a bit but they stayed standing up. Uncle's cheeks went out like balloons and he got redder and redder and redder. Then all of a suddenly, he twizzled round six times and fell on his nose.

I have written down Rule 7 in my Book of Badness. This is it.

RULE 7. DO CHARMING, SNEAKY SMILES.

I think Rule 7 is rubbish. I had to drag Uncle all the way home by his tail.

Yours tiredoutly,

Little

Day 28

Dear Mum and Dad,

Uncle has still got a bad head and tailache. He says he is dying (hem hem) and will not get out of bed. I gave him the bonnet I took from Mister Twister at Borderlands Market. I said, "Here, this will keep your head warm." He put it on, then he told me to depart swiftly, swiftly, so I went exploring in the forest.

I have been thinking about the tents that the cub scouts had. The strings and the pegs were in just right. You could never blow them down, even I could see that and I am just a learner. Are you quite sure you want me to be like Uncle? Sometimes I wonder what is so brilliant about him.

Anyway, soon I came to a new track. It leads to an empty place in the forest made by the

woodcutter cutting down the trees there. And
guess what, there was that girl with the red hood
all by herself with a picnic basket. I thought, Oh
good – more chicken, I am starving. But just
then, her granny came along.

And guess what? All of a suddenly, a cunning
trick jumped in my head! In my mind I saw
Uncle wearing the bonnet I got from Mister
Twister!

I went back to Cunning College running,
running, and I said, "Listen, Uncle, I know how
you can catch a nice tasty little girl with a red
hood. Why not dress up as her granny!"

Uncle said I am the stupidest pupil he has ever had. He said no way will I ever get my BAD badge now.

I am all upset.

Sniff sniff from

Little

Day 29

Dear Mum and Dad,

Uncle jumped out of bed his earliest yet. He said he had thought of a brilliant way to trap that little red-hood girlie, wear a bonnet and pretend to be her granny!

I said, "Uncle, I told you that, that was my idea!!"

He said "SO WHAT?" He said if I was a really clever, cunning bad wolf, I would keep my good ideas to myself and not blab them around. He said, "SO WRITE THAT IN YOUR STUPID BOOK OF BADNESS!"

I must be a slow learner. Still I have written it down. This is it.

RULE 8.   DO NOT BLAB YOUR GOOD IDEAS.

Ho hum from

3 guesses

Day 30

Dear Mum and Dad,

Today I had to help Uncle get dressed up in his bonnet and granny dress and everything. He kept looking in the mirror going, "HUM, YESSS, VERY NICE, I THINK IT SUITS ME." So vain.

At last we got going to the grandma's house about tea time. Guess who went in and had all the fun. Yes, Uncle. He would not let me tie the old lady up or stick her in the wardrobe. He said my job was to stay outside and give a wolf-whistle if any woodcutters came along.

I hid for a bit till Little Red Goodie-hoodie came along with a basket and tip-tapped at the door. you should have heard Uncle's granny-voice, it was rubbish!! Even Smellybreff can do better voices. I would have run a mile if I was that girl. But she is such a sad simple dimple, she walked right in.

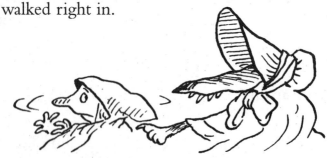

It got so boring just doing nothing. I went off and chased a few snacks for my tea in the forest, but they jumped down their holes, boo, shame. Then I wandered off back to Cunning College.

Big roast supper for Uncle tonight, I 'spect.

But nothing for me.

Yours rumblytumly,

Littly

Day 31

Dear M and D,

Dear oh dear, poor old Uncle. While I was off chasing snacks, the woodcutter came along and whacked him on the bonnet with the back of his axe. Also he split him in 2 and took Little Red Goodie-hoodie out of his tummy.

So guess what, Uncle is not feeling his best today. He said it is all my fault and so I must suffer too.

He made me sew him up and feed him rat soup every 2 hours. I am not allowed to listen to music. And no telly, no fun at all. He kept on and on at me about me being stupid stupid and said I could forget the BAD badge now, *no* chance.

I have been dashing about all over the place finding vinegar and brown paper to wrap Uncle's head in. He will not let me fetch the doctor, he says it costs too much. Also he makes me sit by his bed and keep the flies off him, so boring.

I am a complete failure, so sorry.

Your hopeless cub,

Little

Dear Dum and Mad,

I do not know how to tell you. Something terrible has happened. I have been expelled from Cunning College.

Uncle is not fair. I nursed him and ran around for him. I even fanned him with a cabbage leaf to save using the electric fan. But all of a suddenly, he made me write a letter to Mister Twister at Borderlands Market, like this:

MY DEAR LONG LOST CHUM,

HOW FOOLISH I WAS TO FALL OUT WITH YOU AND SEND YOU AWAY, RUSH TO MY AID AND I WILL REWARD YOU HANSUMLY. I AM AT DEATH'S DOOR, ALL MY NEPHEW'S FAULT.

WHEN I AM BETTER, PERHAPS WE CAN MOVE NEAR A FARM AND WORRY SHEEP TOGETHER.

HURRY. I AM ALL ALONE.
YOUR MELANCHOLY PARTNER,

BEEBEE WOLF

When I finished writing, uncle said,
"GGGGRRRRR! NOW YOU CAN
BLINKING BLUNKING WELL BUZZ OFF. I
AM TOO POOR TO KEEP YOU."

I said, "But, Uncle, I have only got 1 more
Rule of Badness to learn! What about my BAD
badge?"

He said, "TOUGH LUCK. GET OUT. YOU
ARE MUCH TOO EXPENSIVE FOR ME."

Then I made a big mistake. I said, "OO, what
a big miser! I bet you are rich really."

Uncle went crackers. He jumped out of bed.
He yelled, "THAT IS A FLIPPING FLOPPING
BIG WHOPPING LIE!!! WHO TOLD YOU I
HAVE GOT BAGS OF GOLD STUFFED UP
THE …?"

He did not finish saying stuffed up the where.
He just threw cups and saucers at me and
screamed, "GET OUT!!!"

Now I am all by my ownly in Frettnin Forest.

Yours chuckoutly,

L Wolf

Dear Mum and Dad,

Just a short note to say goodbye and sorry. I have let the family down, specially Dad. I am a disgrace to the pack.

Do not worry, I am not coming home badgeless. I am going to hide myself deep in Frettnin Forest and hope that one day my yellow eyes will make friends with the dark and dampness.

Forgive and forget me. I shall change my name and stay far away.

Yours,

Shadow (my secret name)

Dear M and D,

Ahem. Me again. Just when I thought I was stuck being Shadow for ever! Uncle has give me 1 last chance, which is …

He says he might award me my BAD badge. But only if I pass his BIG SURVIVAL TEST.

(A) I must stay alive in Frettnin Forest with no shelter, no provisions, no nothing and

(B) I must bring him back something big and lipsmackerous to eat from the forest.

I have got exactly 1 week to pass this test. Which is a bit too hard for me, I think, but I shall have a go.

Yours once morely,

Littly

PS   Did I ever tell you camping out is my worst thing? Well, I think this might be even ~~worster~~ ~~worser~~ ~~worstest~~ ~~uncomfortabler~~ more nasty.

Dear Mum and Dad,

Just a postcard before I curl up, no post box near. Still it is something to do.

Brrr, frozz here in the open, worse than the tent even. I looked all day for a cave but they have all got huge big grizzly bears in. Also v. little to eat.

Oh yes, that reminds me, I hurt myself trying a new snack today. What do they call them, hedgehogs, is it? Talk about hot, it really burnt my mouth. How was I know you are supposed to peel them first?

Anyway, no way was that snack lipsmackerous. Dear oh flip, I do not think I will *ever* pass Uncle's BIG TEST.

Bbbrrr.

Your chilly boy,

Little

Dear M and D,

As you can see from the above address, I have moved. Not that it is any more comfy, I am wedged in like a tight nut in a shell. Dear oh dear, what a rubbish shelter, and only a few grubs to chew.

At least the rain has stopped. About time because my fur has gone soggy like a rat in a gutter. It makes you feel all spooky when it stops pattering on the leaves.

I thought I heard something rustle in the bushes outside just now. Maybe it is Uncle come to check me out. But he would not bother, so who is it????

Yours Oo-erly,

Littly

Lakeside Camp
Day 37

Dear Mum and Dad,

Oh no, trapped!!! Now who is the sad simple dimple? Me! The whistly pack leader will put me in a zoo tomorrow, I know it. And I cannot even stand my bedroom, let alone cages!!

You know I said about rustling? Well, it was 2 cub scouts crawling through the bushes. I thought, Funny, what are they doing in the forest? Then I thought, Yum yum, I am starving and scouts look more lipsmackerous than hedgehogs any day. I will pounce on them silently, eat 1 and save the other for Uncle. Then I will pass the BIG TEST, yippee.

Sad to say, my cunning plan went a bit wrong. P'raps it was my rumbling tum, I do not know, but all of a suddenly 1 cub scout turned round and saw me lurking. He said, "I say, old chap, you do not look quite well. Can we assist you in some way?"

All of a suddenly, everything went black and when I woke up in their camp, oh no! I was zipped up to my chin in a padded bag and laid down inside a tent! Then the whistly pack leader came along saying, "Oh dear, sonny jim, you are skinny as a rake, we had better fatten you up."

Do they have fat wolf cubs in zoos? Oo-er, maybe they are fattening me up for the cooking pot!!! Please do not tell Smells or Yeller if I end up as stew.

Yours capturedly,

Little

Dear Mum and Dad,

Burn my last letter,
I am *sooo* lucky!

I am not on the menu, I am a guest
(somebody you have to stay). That zippy bag was
not a trap, it was for sleeping, hmmm cosy! They
put me in it for *first aid*!

And listen to this bit, the pack leader says they
are going to return me to the wild as soon as I
am ready!! BUT *not before I have had loads and
loads of grub to build up my strength!*

I have just had stew, potatoes and bakebeans.
Brilliant, specially the bakebeans, I *love* them, kiss
kiss!

The boys who found me in the forest are called Dave and Sanjay. They were out playing the Wide Game which is trying to creep back to the camp by the lake without your friends seeing you. Today they are going to teach it to me and also something called Campcraft, which is great because true I am quite crafty, but my camping is rubbish. I aim to get good and surprise Uncle.

Nip Smellybreff for me and tell him not long now before he sees his ~~hansum~~ handsome brother (this is me, he is the ugly one going boo-hoo!!!).

Yours,

Tubby tum (get it?)

Dear Mum and Dad,

Today we did putting up a shelter; how to stay alive if you get lost; making a shoe-rack out of sticks and string; lighting a fire and nkots (is that right?). Now I know just the right nkot for tying up grandmothers and baby brothers, so watch out, Smells! Tomorrow the pack leader says he will show us mapping and compass-work and tracking. Handy for a wolf, eh? A lot better than Uncle Bigbad's lessons, if you ask me (do not tell him). Anyway, I can pass Uncle's BIG TEST easy cheesy now, I bet.

And guess what, if you join the Cub Scouts properly you can get *loads* of badges!! But there is 1 problem, Dave says you have to make a Cub Scout promise. So tough on me because how can you be BAD *and* make a promise? It is too goody-goody.

Probably I shall stay here 1 more day and then go back to the forest. This is my plan: set up a brilliant camp and wait for Uncle to come and be impressed. My only small problem is finding something big and lipsmackerous to eat, but maybe something will turn up.

Then I can pass my BIG TEST, finish properly at Cunning College, get my BAD badge and you can all be proud of me. Tell yeller to get ready because we are going to have a wicked time when I get home! And he will say, "Hello, Little Wolf, cor, you are just like your Uncle, only badder."

Arrroooo!

~~klaos~~ ~~tonks~~ nokes

Littly

PS   Sanjay says there is a k in nots which sounds daft but I have written one in case.

Dear Mum and Dad,

Lots to tell you. It's a good thing I like
writing. Guess what, the Pack Leader is an Akela,
same as Dad!!

Cub Scouts are great! Did you know you can
do *loads* of badges if you join. Akela said if I
stayed, I could study for Camper, Explorer,
Navigator, Book Reader, etc. They even have
one called Animal Lover. I said, Oh arrooooo, I
am an Animal Lover, I love rabbit rolls. But Akela
said, Animal Lover is not an eating badge. Ah
well. Pity.

I am really good at putting up tents now and
the Wide Game and telling stories round the
campfire. Today I told all about Uncle and
Cunning College and the 9 Rules of Badness,
and how important it is for me to get my BAD
badge.

Everybody asked me what are the 9 Rules of Badness. I said, "Sorry, I only know 8, will they do?" and they said, "Yes, tell us." So I said,

" 1. Huff and puff a lot.
2. Say loads of rude words.
3. Fib your head off.
4. Blow everyone else.
5. If it squeaks, eat it.
6. Do your dirtiest every day.
7. Do charming.
8. Do not blab your good ideas."

Dave said, "That is interesting because the Cub Scout rules are just the opposite, and they are:
1. Do your best.
2. Think of others.
3. Do good turns."

I said, "har har, good joke, Dave!" Then Akela said, "So, sonny jim, was it that big bad fellow who tried to blow our tents down taught you all those nasty rules?"

So I said, "Yes, it was Uncle Bigbad."

So Akela said, "Well, I am sorry, sonny jim, but I think your uncle should not be a teacher. He should be locked away. He is a cruel, savage brute."

I said, "Gosh, thanks a lot, Akela. Uncle would be so happy to hear you say those kind words!"

Yours newsily,

L

Dear Mum and Dad,

Today is my best day so far since I started having adventures. Guess what, I have made HISTORY!

This is what happened. I was feeling a bit sad and sorry because today was my last day with the cub scouts. I was in my tent packing my rucksack in the cub scout way (without pointy things sticking in your back). Then Sanjay came and said I was wanted.

The cub scouts all made a ring and I stood in the middle. Then Akela said, "Just before you go, sonny jim, we want you to take 1 or 2 things to remember us by." He said, "You have made the last few days very special for Lakeside Camp. Because you are the first real wolf cub we have met. We are proud to be part of your Great Adventure, and thus and therefore, we would like to make a presentation. So here is your special CUB SCOUT ADVENTURE AWARD with certificate and badge."

Can you *beleeeeve* it, a BADGE! At last!!! Plus they gave me a load of provisions including chocklit fingers, potty noodles and 3 WHACKING big tins of bakebeans (canteen size), because they are my favourite.

Arrrooooooooo

from The Adventurer

Dear Mum and Dad,

I am deep in the forest where it is so dark and dismal you would not beleeeeeve! Even the bats wear glasses (only kidding). But I am not scared 1 bit!

Have made this *excellent* shelter out of sticks and leaves (a bivouac if you want to know the proper cub scout word, hem hem). Also I have got a fire going with 1 match (stones all round to keep it from spreading, v. important).

I am so warm and cosy, it is brilliant! And guess what I have cooked? Alphabetti spaghetti, it comes in tins. I will bring you some and show you how to open them. There you are, I have done a SMELLYBREFF in spaghetti and stuck it on the page for him. Good, eh?

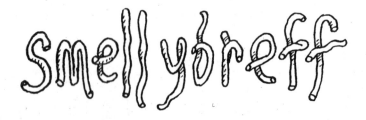

I am just waiting till midnight so that I can creep back to Cunning College and surprise Uncle. Because I have passed my BIG TEST. I am still alive after 1 week and I have got some lipsmackerous stuff for him to eat.

So DYB DYB DOB DOB to you!

Yours campcraftily,

Little

Day 43

Dear Mum and Dad,

Big shock!! Arrived back at Cunning College and found Uncle all tied up with rope and skinnier than ever! Cunning College was a mess, desks tipped over, furniture upset, rubbish all over. He said, "GGRRR! UNTIE ME, SWIFTLY, SWIFTLY, WHERE HAVE YOU BEEN?" I said, "Having an adventure. Where is Mister Twister?"

He said, "HE ATTACKED ME! HE TIED ME UP! HE WAS TRYING TO FIND MY MONEYBAGS AND NOW HE HAD WRECKED MY SCHOOL. THE BLINKING BLUNKER!"

I said, "What moneybags, Uncle? I thought you were poor."

He said, "GGGRRR! SILENCE, SQUIRT! CLEAN UP THIS PLACE AND GET ME SOMETHING TO EAT! I MUST LIE DOWN ON THE COUCH."

I said, "OK, I will tidy up and I will give you something lipsmackerous to eat. So now I have passed the BIG TEST will you give me a BAD badge after?"

Uncle said, "WHAT A MAGNIFICENT LITTLE PUPIL YOU ARE. OF COURSE YOU SHALL HAVE A BAD BADGE! BUT FOOD FIRST, BADGE AFTERWARDS."

So exciting! Must stop now because lots of work to be done.

Yours with a big  Arrrooooo!

Little

Cunning College for Brute Beasts

Day 44

Dear Mum and Dad,

What a big cheater Uncle is! Now I am all down and dumpy again!

I cleaned up the whole college, picked up, swept up, scrubbed up, mopped up and put away, phew. Then Uncle just gobbled up all my chocklit fingers and he wolfed down my potty noodles. He is such a greedy guts he did not bother to cook them or take them out of their plastic potties. Then he had a long long zizz on the couch.

When he woke up this morning he said he was starving hungry again. He bashed me with the board rubber and made me cook him breakfast. I said, "But I have passed my test! I lived in the forest by myself and I stayed alive. Plus I gave you something big and lipsmackerous for tea yesterday. So give me my BAD badge and let me go!"

He said, "OH, CERTAINLY CERTAINLY, CROSS MY HEART, STRAIGHT AFTER BREAKFAST, YOU CAN TRUST *ME*!"

I am down and dumpy because now I will have to cook him some of my special bakebeans and I was saving them, 1 for me, 1 for you and Smells, and 1 for yeller.

More later on. 3 boos for Uncle.

Little

CUNNING COLLEGE FOR BRUTE BEASTS

Dear Mum and Dad,

This is a bit sad but no presents for anybody. Sorry.

After I lit the fire, I put on the great big pot and filled it right up to the brim with my canteen-size tin of bakebeans. When the beans were nice and hot, Uncle went extra dribbly and he said, "GET A BIG BIG SPOON! FEED ME FEED ME, SWIFTLY, SWIFTLY!"

I said, "Careful, Uncle, bakebeans are gorgeous but don't eat too fast. Look at what the label says. Beware of the jumping beanbangs!"

But he would not look, he would not listen. He got huffy and puffy and he threw the spoon in the corner. He yelled, "TOO SMALL! GET THE LADLE AND FEED ME FEED ME, SWIFTLY, SWIFTLY!" So I did. He swallowed the lot in 35 secs. Then he licked his lips and his voice went all weak and he said, "What about 1 more tin?"

So number 2 tin that I was saving for Yeller went into the pot, canteen-size again. When the bakebeans were hotted up, I fed them to Uncle with the ladle. Talk about a quick eater, it was like stoking the boiler. Uncle said (weak voice), "Just 1 more tiny tin?"

I said, "But they are my treat for my mum and dad and Smellybreff, I am saving them. I went to take them home with my BAD badge so they can be proud of me. Besides, remember the label. Beware of the jumping beanbangs!"

But he said, "GGGGGRRR, WHO CARES
ABOUT BLUNKING BLARSTED
BEANBANGS! GET THE COAL SHOVEL
AND FEED ME, SWIFTLY, SWIFTLY!!!"

So number 3 tin that I was saving for you and
Smells went into the pot, the biggest tin of
bakebeans you can get.

Uncle opened his mouth wide as wide and I
shovelled in all the bakebeans with the coal
shovel, swiftly, swiftly.

Then he smacked his horrible lips and he
rolled his horrible eyes and he said, "NOT
ENOUGH, I MUST HAVE MORE! DASH
BACK TO LAKESIDE CAMP AND GET
LASHINGS MORE BAKEBEANS, SWIFTLY,
SWIFTLY!"

I said, "But Uncle, My BAD badge, you promised!"

He said, "HAR HAR YOU SAD SUCKER! IT IS TIME I TOLD YOU RULE NUMBER 9. AND RULE NUMBER 9 IS …

NEVER TRUST A BIG
BAD WOLF!"

I wish I had thought of that before.

Yours badgelessly,

Littly

Day 45

Dear Mother and Father,

Um what can I say, Uncle had a slight accident last night.

So I shall be quite busy burying him etc.

Please excuse short note.

Love

Little

Dear Mum and Dad,

Gosh what a tiring day yesterday. Soon after the accident, Akela and the cub scouts came. They helped me look for Uncle. We searched all morning but the only thing we found was his whiskers and his bonnet. So it did not take long digging a grave, very small. But it took ages carving a nice message on his gravestone, Akela said it is quite good rhyming and true, what do you think.

> Bigbad Wolf is dead at last he died of eating beans too fast

This afternoon, found his gold BAD badge, it was hanging from the rafters.

More tomorrow.

Yours wornly,

Little

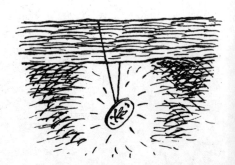

Day 47

Dear Mum and Dad,

I forgot to tell you how Uncle died. Sorry, I was a bit busy.

It was a suddenly thing. Because after Uncle scoffed all the bakebeans, suddenly there was this great big loud noise in the night, it made me jump. I thought Oh blow, Uncle is riding his motorbike round the furniture. But no, it was not a motorbike, it was just him jumping round holding his tummy, going POP-POP-POP-KERBANG! POP-POP-POP KERBANG!!!

I said, "Oh no, Uncle, you have got the jumping beanbangs from scoffing all those beans with the shovel! Best to stay in bed and open the window. But please, Uncle, whatever you do, do not go near the fire."

But he would not listen, he went mad. He said, "GET ME A LOG TO LUMP YOUR HEAD WITH!" And his great big eyes were rolling and his great big teeth were shining and his great big kerbangs were kerbanging.

I said, "Please keep away from the fire, Uncle!"

He said, "YOU CAN'T TRICK ME WITH YOUR PLEASES AND YOUR GOODY-GOODY WAYS." And he chased me round and round. Then he said his last words. He said,

"I'LL BOOM, I'LL BANG, I'LL BASH YOU FOR THIS!!! YOU BOOM YOU BANG YOU *BAD* LITTLE WOLF!!!"

Those were his last words because then he bent down by the fire to pick up a log to lump me with and

He exploded. Shame, eh? (In a way.) That is when the chimney fell over. It is lying in the garden now.

Yours sorry about not mentioning beforely,

L

Dear Mr and Mrs Moneybags and
   Baby Posh,

Aha, tricked you! You thought this letter was for somebody else I bet! But no, you ARE posh and moneybags now. Because, guess what, Uncle was telling big fat fibs about being poor!! (Rule 3.)

I was in the garden just now, feeling like mucking about for a bit. The chimney was lying among the flowers. So I thought, I know, I will just have a quick game of chimney sweeps, I like getting sooty. And in I crawled. It was very funny and squeezy. But the soot was so tickly, it made my nose tickle. So I went Ah-hah-hah-TishINKLE!

And do you know what the TishINKLE was? It was GOLD!!! BAGS AND BAGS OF IT!!! So

THAT is where Uncle had stuffed it. Up the chimney!!!

Now we are *RICH*.

I have drawn me with Uncle's gold and his big gold BAD badge on my chest. I have awarded it to myself.

Yours deservingly,

L B Wolf (B for BAD, get it?)

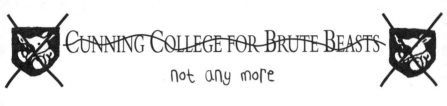

Midwood
Beastshire

Day 49

Dear Mum and Dad,

Do not worry, I shall be home soon. I am nearly ready but not quite.

I 'spect you will say Boohoo what is up? What is keeping our boy? He is rich, we are proud of him, he knows the 9 Rules of Badness, he has got a gold BAD badge. Plus he hates being away from home, it is his worst thing. So whyo whyo Y does he not zoom back to his nice smelly old lair?

Answer – ADVENTURES, I love them yum yum kiss kiss!! They are my best thing now. I want loads more. BUT (big but) I do not like

1. going round and round in circles getting lost.
2. rain, ants etc down my neck.
3. falling-down tents.
4. problems chasing snacks, etc.
5. big **fibbers** tricking me and being nasty to me.

So I am joining the cub scouts properly. Yes, I have decided to do the promise and everything. Akela is going to bring Dave and Sanjay and the rest of the cub scouts to camp on the college lawn. Tomorrow they are going to help me study for my Navigator badge and my Explorer badge.

Then I shall be able to find my way home, and no mistakes!

See you soonly,

LBW

ADVENTURE ACADEMY

Dear Mum and Dad,

I have changed my mind, I am not coming back to the Lair.

BUT do not howl sadly, because I am having such a good time doing my Navigator and Explorer badges. Plus now I have decided something. I do not wish to be like Uncle Bigbad. He was really Uncle Bigsad (get it?) because he had no friends. he was all huff and puff and hot air, so not surprising he went off bang, eh?

When I grow up I want to be ME, not just some big old horrible wolf that nobody trusts.

So guess what, I have decided to use some of the bags of money to start a new college in Frettnin Forest. And it will be called

Smellybreff and Yeller must come straight away. They can be teachers with me and it will be the best fun school in the world. Ever!!

Also I have made the cellar nice and smelly. That means you can come and be happy hibernaters ever after!! So

Arrrooooooo.

From

Little Bad Wolf

PS   I am sending you 1 bag of money for fares etc. Buy Smells some fake blood, some itchy powder, a whoopy cushion and get a pretend arrow through the head for Yeller. From now on, the tricks are on me !!!!!

DA DAA

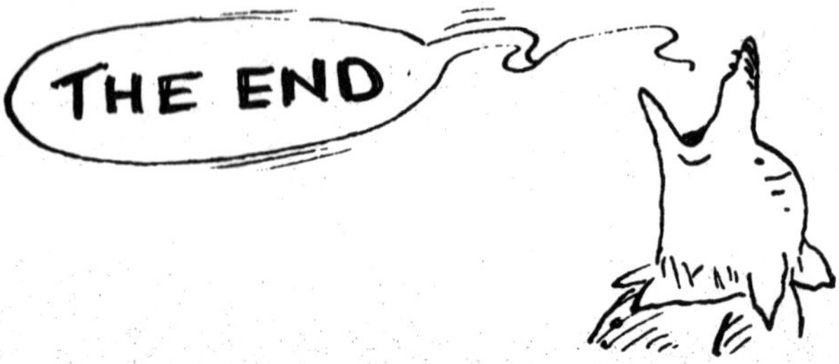
THE END

MORE THAN A STORY
CONTENTS PAGE

Dear Reader

I am a Bad Badge holder no_W , so cannot sa**y**
thank **y**ou, sorr**y**. Still, here is a '_Well done **y**ou'
for reading m**y** letters, plus a merci (French).

It is k_Wite nice being back at the lair. I think
Smells is more happ**y** than Mum and Dad. I bet
it is just becuz I am all rich no_W _With Uncle
Bigbad's gold going chinkle in m**y** pocket. I
think soon I _Will have to do some short tricks
on Smells to teach him about me being top cub,
plus him being naught but a pain**y** fluffball.

Talking of doing tricks, here is a rich re_Ward
*//*for you*//*. **wh**y oh Y? you ask. **w**hat have
I dun to derserve re_Wards? Ans_Wer: It is becuz
of all **y**our hard reading of m**y** posh book. Did
you notice it is a classick no_W, hem hem? (Like
carsick, onl**y** more fun.)

Here **y**ou are then, have sum puzzles, plus a
load of _Wolfl**y** secrets, tips, puzuls (cannot spell
it) etc. Also, here are sum shocking tricks so
people _Will think, oo-er, **y**ou are more cunning
than Uncle Bigbad, even.

Yours classickl**y**

L **w**olf (author)

SECRET MESSAGES

Invisible Ink
Little Wolf was scared that Uncle Bigbad would read his letters. So he wrote them in invisible ink! He got a lemon and squeezed the juice. He found a little stick and dipped it in the juice. Then he wrote his letter. When it dried, it looked like a blank sheet of paper. But at home, Smellybreff put it on the radiator and the writing magically showed up:

Dear Smells
I am writing this becos I don't want Uncle Bigbad to know that I think he is mean and horrible. He might be glad. Ask Mum to send me some mice pies. Write 'soap' on the packet. Then Uncle won't open it.

Yours bruvly

Little Wolf

If you haven't got lemon juice, you can use milk or vinegar, instead.

Wet and Dry

Another way of writing a secret message is to take two sheets of paper, one damp and one dry. Write your message with a ballpoint pen on the dry, top sheet. Press hard but don't go through the paper. Tear up the top sheet. (You don't want to leave any clues!) Dry the bottom sheet, which now looks blank. Your friend can lightly paint over it and the message will appear.

Who shouted 'Stinky!' at the Big Bad Wolf?
Little Rude Riding Hood.

Clever Code

You could use a secret code. Smells has sent a message back to Little. What is it?

D	O	A	E
A	F	L	P
D	F	L	I
S	E	T	E
C	D	H	S

Clue: read down the boxes.

What do you get if you cross a snowman with a wolf?

Frost bite.

TOP FIVE WOLF FACTS

1 Most wolves are grey and about the size of a very large dog and have very big feet – about 10 cm wide and 13 cm long!

2 They can run for many miles at about 5 mph but over short distances they can sprint at up to 40 mph. Much faster than the average human!

3 They eat deer, moose, elk and small creatures such as insects, mice or rabbits. They almost never attack humans, in spite of their fierce reputation.

4 Humans are their greatest enemy because people want to travel and live in the wilderness which is the wolves' home.

5 There really was a little boy in India who was brought up by wolves and he was the inspiration for Mowgli, in *The Jungle Book* by Rudyard Kipling.

AN IN-DEPTH LOOK AT WOLVES

Where do wolf cubs live?

Mother wolf has her babies in a den, which is a nice, safe cave or burrow in the ground.

The babies are tiny and blind, but they grow fast. They love playing and as soon as they can see, they spend their time in games with their brothers and sisters, learning all the skills they'll need to survive. Both mother and father wolf help to look after the babies and when they are old enough they join the pack.

Arrooo! Do wolves talk to each other?

Yes they do! They howl, growl and bark, and whimper.

People used to think that wolves howled at the moon, but this is probably because they move about in the moonlight – so that is when they are most likely to howl.

They *howl* when they want to make their voices carry over a long distance.

They *bark* if a stranger comes into their territory.

They *whimper* to say 'hello' or when they meet a more powerful wolf.

Are wolves like dogs?

Yes and no.

Dogs are different from their wild relations, but they do still do some of the same things.

Different:

Wolves have to hunt to live, so they have stronger jaws for catching food.

They also have bigger feet for travelling long distances.

Same:

Dogs use body language like wolves. They tuck their tail between their legs when they are afraid or want to run away. They prick up their ears when they hear something interesting.

Dogs like to roll in something smelly. So do wolves! People think this is because wolves want to hide their own smell so that they can creep up on other animals, unnoticed.

What do you call a wolf with cotton wool in his ears?

Anything you like. He can't hear you!

LITTLE WOLF'S PUZZLE PAGES

Word Fun

If I can turn BAD into DAB and WOLF into FLOW, what can I turn DRAWER into?

When you add 'bad' to these letters, you get something that Little Wolf really wants.

Answer: _ _ _ _ GE

Puzzling Prizes

Little Wolf went to the theme park with the cubs and tried to knock down the piles of tins. He managed to knock down all four piles. What did he win?

STAIPN

APC

EIC-MEACR

ANABAN

Who Comes Out at Night?

Some animals move about at night, especially at dawn and dusk because that's when they can find food most easily and because it's not safe for them to be out during the day. These animals have a very good sense of smell and special eyes which can see better in low light than humans can. Bats even have built in radar, so they can 'see' in the dark..

B	O	L	H	W	V	G	M	O
A	O	I	E	A	O	O	W	T
D	R	O	D	J	U	L	A	A
G	A	N	G	S	P	C	F	R
E	G	L	E	O	P	A	R	D
R	N	F	H	T	I	G	E	R
T	A	B	O	V	I	F	O	X
R	K	F	G	O	P	P	I	H

Can you find all the animals listed below in the wordsearch. Look up, down, forwards, backwards and diagonally.

OWL, BAT, RAT, MOUSE, HEDGEHOG, BADGER, CAT, FOX, WOLF, HIPPO, LEOPARD, LION, TIGER, KANGAROO

What do you do if you find a big bad wolf in your bed?

Sleep somewhere else!

Scary Circles

Clues:

1 A very little child

2 The opposite of fat

3 Where Little is scared he'll be locked up

4 I like an ice ---- in my drink

5 Wolf cubs love to do this.

6 The opposite of narrow?

Copy out the target and answer the clues. Write them in the target, starting with the first letter in the outer ring and moving inwards. Each answer has 4 letters. Now read the shaded ring to find someone that Little is scared of.

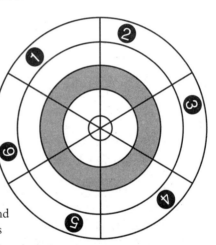

Why are wolves like cards?
They come in packs.

Scrambled Serpent

Unscramble this serpent, to find something
Little Wolf likes.

Help! I'm Lost!

Help baby wolfie find his way home to the den.

START

FINISH

What do you call a lost wolf?
A where-wolf!

SURVIVING IN FRETTNIN FOREST

Little Wolf makes a compass

If you are stuck in the forest, like Little Wolf, and you don't know which way to go, you need a compass to stop you wandering round in circles.

You need:

A needle (GET AN ADULT TO HELP!)

A glass of water.

A small cork

A strong magnet.

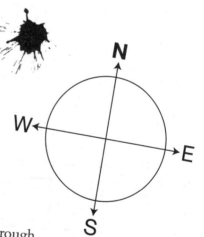

1. First, rub the magnet along the needle about 40 times. (Always rub in the same direction. Don't go backwards and forwards.)

2. Now push the needle through the cork. (GET AN ADULT TO HELP!)

3. Put the needle into the cup of water. It will float and once it has come to rest, it will point north–south.

Little Wolf makes a den

Little Wolf's idea of a good den was squeezing into a hollow tree, until he met the boy scouts and they showed him how to built a shelter, or bivouac, as they called it.

Here's what to do :

1. Find something strong and solid to build your shelter against. A fallen tree trunk, a rock or a wall would all be good.

2. Collect about 10 or 12 thin leafy branches. Lean them up at an angle against the tree trunk, rock or wall. Make sure that they are secure and won't fall.

3. Lie down under the branches to check that you've made your shelter long enough to cover you.

4. Finally, add a layer of leaves, grass and moss — whatever you can find — to cover the branches, and make it as cosy as possible.

What's the best way to speak
to a big bad wolf?
From a long way away.

GAMES TO PLAY AT CAMP

Little Wolf likes sitting round the campfire but best of all is when it's time for a game.

Wolf's Footsteps

One person is Mr Wolf and stands about 10 metres away with his back to everyone. Everyone else calls out, "What's the time, Mr Wolf?" trying to creep up on the 'wolf' at the same time.

Mr Wolf replies, "One o'clock" and whirls around. If he sees anyone moving, he sends them back to the starting line. If 'Mr Wolf' senses that someone is getting close to him, he can whirl around yelling, "Dinner time" and chase everyone back to the starting line. If he catches anyone they are out of the game.

But if anyone manages to touch the wolf on the shoulder before he turns around, they have won and it is their turn to be Mr Wolf.

What card game does a big bad wolf like to play?
Snap.

Wolf's Supper

Everyone sits round in a circle and throws a dice. The first person to get a 6 puts on a big heavy coat, scarf and woolly hat. Once they are dressed they can start supper, which is a bar of chocolate (or an apple, pear and banana). The problem is that they have to eat it with a knife and fork! They aren't allowed to use their fingers.

Meanwhile, everyone else is throwing the dice and as soon as someone else gets a 6, it is their turn to put on the coat, scarf and hat and start tucking in until the next person with a 6 comes to take over…

Make a BAD Badge

Make a gold BAD badge and wear it proudly, like Little Wolf.

You need:

A circle of cardboard, as big as you want!

Gold/red and black paint

Safety pin and sticky tape, or a length of string or ribbon

1. Paint a gold or red background for the badge, let it dry, and then decorate the badge in black. Paint BAD in big letters.
2. Tape the safety pin securely to the back of the badge and pin it to your chest.
3. Or cut a hole in the top of the badge and thread the ribbon through to wear around your neck.

Use this 'medallion' BAD badge for the wolf games! Mr Wolf can wear it for Wolf's Footsteps, and it can be something else to put on before wolfing down Wolf's Supper.

ANSWERS

Clever Code

DAD SCOFFED ALL THE PIES

*Who Comes
Out at Night?*

Word Fun

REWARD
BADGE

B	O	L	H	W	V	G	M	O
A	O	I	E	A	O	O	W	T
D	R	O	D	J	U	L	A	A
G	A	N	G	S	P	C	F	R
E	G	L	E	O	P	A	R	D
R	N	F	H	T	I	G	E	R
T	A	B	O	V	I	F	O	X
R	K	F	G	O	P	P	I	H

Puzzling Prizes

PAINTS
CAP
ICE-CREAM
BANANA

Scary Circles

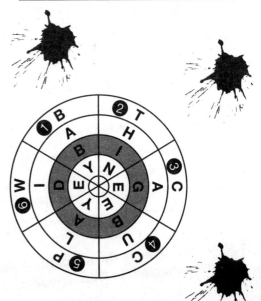

Scrambled Serpent

PRESENT